This book should be returned to any branch of the
Lancashire County Library on or before the date shown

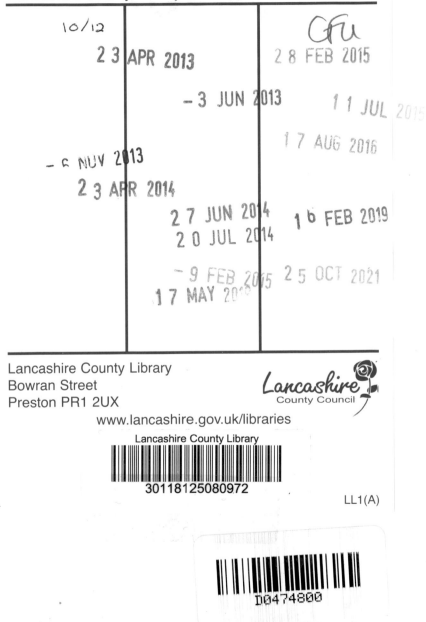

10/12

23 APR 2013

28 FEB 2015

- 3 JUN 2013

11 JUL 2015

17 AUG 2016

- 6 NOV 2013

23 APR 2014

27 JUN 2014

16 FEB 2019

20 JUL 2014

- 9 FEB 2015

25 OCT 2021

17 MAY 2015

Lancashire County Library
Bowran Street
Preston PR1 2UX
www.lancashire.gov.uk/libraries

Lancashire
County Council

For Lawrence & Matilda

Bloomsbury Publishing, London, Berlin and New York

First published in Great Britain in 2009 by Bloomsbury Publishing Plc
36 Soho Square, London, W1D 3QY

Text and illustrations copyright © Dosh Archer 2009
The moral right of the author/illustrator has been asserted

A CIP catalogue record of this book is available from the British Library

ISBN 978 0 7475 9764 3

Printed in Singapore by Tien Wah Press

1 3 5 7 9 10 8 6 4 2

All papers used by Bloomsbury Publishing are natural, recyclable products made from
wood grown in well-managed forests. The manufacturing processes conform to the
environmental regulations of the country of origin

www.bloomsbury.com/childrens
www.urgencyemergency.com

URGENCY EMERGENCY!
Choking Wolf

Dosh Archer

BLOOMSBURY

LONDON BERLIN NEW YORK

It was a busy day at City Hospital. Doctor Glenda was writing something important on the wallchart. Nurse Percy was helping someone in a red coat who was crying because she couldn't find her grandma.

Just then the ambulance arrived.

'Urgency Emergency! We have a wolf here who is choking! Choking wolf coming through!'

'Let me examine him,' said
Doctor Glenda.

'It's just as I thought – he is choking. There is something caught in his throat, which means the air cannot get to his lungs. We must remove whatever is stuck in there. Nurse Percy, I need your help!'

Nurse Percy was hiding under the bed, shaking with fear.

'He may be a wolf,' said Doctor
Glenda, 'but he is still our patient.
He only has minutes to live!

Nurse Percy, can you
overcome your fear of wolves
and help me save him?'

Nurse Percy pulled himself together. 'Good man,' said Doctor Glenda.

'Wait,' cried Nurse Percy. 'What is that noise? Where is it coming from?'

It was coming from
inside Wolf.

'It's more serious than I feared,'
said Doctor Glenda. 'It may not be
something stuck in his throat –
it may be some*one*.'

She shone a light into Wolf's mouth so she could look down his throat.

'I can see something,' she said.
'We must get him or her out.'

Doctor Glenda slapped Wolf on the
back quite hard three times.

Wolf spluttered and gasped,
but nothing happened.

'Nurse Percy,' cried Doctor Glenda, 'I need your help. I have to stand behind Wolf and squeeze his tummy, so that whoever is down there will pop out.'

Nurse Percy made Wolf stand up.

Doctor Glenda reached round his middle and squeezed.

Wolf made weird noises and his eyes seemed to be popping out of his head, but nothing came out of his mouth.

Doctor Glenda tried again.

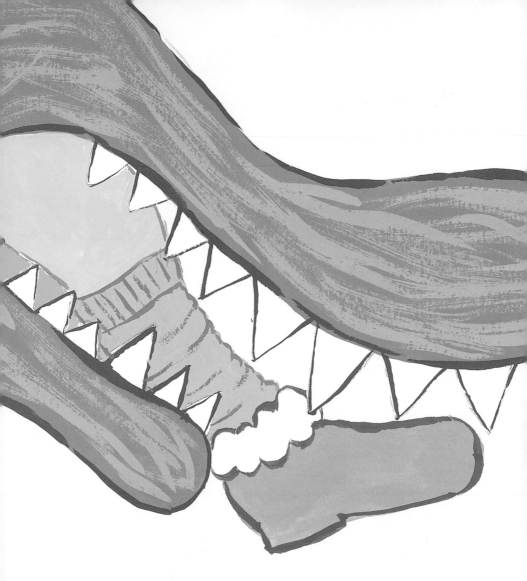

Bleugh! Something poked out of
Wolf's mouth.

'It's a pair of slippers!' cried Nurse
Percy. 'With someone wearing
them!'

'Once more,' said Doctor Glenda.
She squeezed again and out popped
. . . Grandma!

She was damp and a bit chewed at the edges, but otherwise OK.

'It's the missing grandma!' cried
Nurse Percy. 'Wolf tried to eat
her. That is against the law.
Quick, call the police!'

Wolf tried to escape, but he was too weak from lack of breath to put up much of a fight. Nurse Percy and the team held him down . . .

. . . until the police came to take him away.

'I can never thank you enough,'
said Grandma.

'All in a day's work,' said
Doctor Glenda.

Grandma and her little
granddaughter went off happily.

It was another good job done by Doctor Glenda and her team.

Enjoy more madcap first readers in the
URGENCY EMERGENCY! series . . .